I DIG

Joe Cepeda

I Like to Read®

HOLIDAY HOUSE • NEW YORK

Copyright © 2019 by Joe Cepeda • All Rights Reserved • HOLIDAY HOUSE is registered in the U.S. Patent and Trademark Office.
Printed and bound in October 2018 at Tien Wah Press, Johor Bahru, Johor, Malaysia. • The artwork was created with Corel Painter and Adobe Workshop.
www.holidayhouse.com • First Edition • 1 3 5 7 9 10 8 6 4 2
Library of Congress Cataloging-in-Publication Data • Names: Cepeda, Joe, author, illustrator. • Title: I dig / Joe Cepeda.
Description: First edition. | New York : Holiday House, [2019] | Series: I like to read | Summary:
"At the beach, a boy digs a tunnel where he finds a crab, starfish, and best of all, a dog"— Provided by publisher.
Identifiers: LCCN 2018006869 | ISBN 9780823439751 (hardcover) • Subjects: | CYAC: Excavation—Fiction. | Beaches—Fiction.
Classification: LCC PZ7.C3184 Iaf 2019 | DDC [E]—dc23 LC record available at https://lccn.loc.gov/2018006869

For Lou Henry Whittier Elementary School,
Whittier, California

Look.

Look.

Look.

I dig.

I see a crab.

I see stars.

I see a dog.

I go.

I go up.

He is up.

I lie down.

I see stars.